JULIAN AT THE WEDDING

To Danny

First published 2020 by Walker Books Ltd, 87 Vauxhall Walk, London SE11 5HJ
© 2020 Jessica Love • The moral rights of the author-illustrator have been
asserted • This book has been typeset in Godlike • Printed in China
All rights reserved. • British Library Cataloguing in Publication Data is
available • ISBN 978-1-4063-9748-2 • 10 9 8 7 6 5 4 3 2 1

Jessica Love

WALKER BOOKS
AND SUBSIDIARIES
LONDON · BOSTON · SYDNEY · AUCKLAND

This is Julian.

And this is Marisol.

Today they are going to be in a wedding.

Those are the brides, and that's their dog, Gloria.

A wedding is a party for love.

"Let's go," whispers Marisol.

"It's a fairy house," whispers Julian.

"Marisol?"

"Oh."

"Uh-oh!"

Julian has an idea...

"I got dirty."

"Yes, darling, but now you have wings!"

"There you are!"

And then there was dancing.